PRINCES & PRINCESSES

SEVEN TALES OF ENCHANTMENT

ORCHARD BOOKS

338 Euston Road, London, NW1 3BH

Orchard Books Australia

Level 17/207 Kent Street, Sydney NSW 2000

ISBN 978 1 84616 590 0

This edition first published in 2007 by Orchard Books

This edition © Orchard Books 2007

Text and illustrations © individual authors and illustrators; see acknowledgements

The authors and illustrators have asserted their rights

under the Copyright, Designs and Patents Act, 1988.

A CIP catalogue record for this book is available from the British Library.

10 9 8 7 6 5 4 3 2 1

Printed in China

Orchard Books is a division of Hachette Children's Books, an Hachette Livre UK company.

PRINCES & PRINCESSES

SEVEN TALES OF ENCHANTMENT

ORCHARD BOOKS

CONTENTS

CINDERELLA

GERALDINE MCCAUGHREAN

ANGELA BARRETT

✶ ✶ ✶ ✶ ✶ ✶ ✶ ✶ ✶ ✶ ✶ ✶ ✶ ✶ ✶

"CINDERELLA! That's what we'll call you. Cinderella! Because you're always sitting warming your feet in the cinders instead of working! Lazy, idle, good-for-nothing Cinderella!"

Once upon a time those were the squeaks and squawks that flew about in the big house on the hill. Three sisters lived there with their father, but you would have thought there were only two sisters and one scullery maid, for the two older ones, Gouda and Gorgonzola, treated the youngest with such dreadful unkindness. "Only a *stepsister*," they said. "Hardly a sister at all." And they made her do all the housework and fetch and carry for them without ever a word of thanks in return.

One day there was even more work than usual. There was to be a royal ball at the palace. The king wished his son, the prince, to meet every lady of noble birth and from

among them choose a wife! That is why Gouda and Gorgonzola had been trying on different dresses and hats all morning, strutting vainly up and down in front of the mirror. The effort quite wore them out. They had only enough energy left to bully Cinderella and quarrel between themselves. She could hear them overhead in the warm living room. Cinderella sighed a deep sigh.

A voice behind her said, "Listen to them. Hammer and tongs. I wish they wouldn't."

"Father! I didn't hear you come in!" Cinderella ran to get her father some tea and he sat by the kitchen fire to drink it.

"I wish they wouldn't be so unkind to you, my dear," he said. Cinderella smiled. "I wish things could be as they were in the old days: just you, your mother and I."

Cinderella might have asked then why he did not stand up to his stepdaughters, why he let them behave so badly. Her father was not the bravest of men, but she loved him very much. "There, there, don't fret, Father," she said, and patted his shoulder with one hand while she stirred the soup for lunch with the other. She had long ago realised there was no one in the world to save her from Gouda and Gorgonzola.

"Cinderella! The door! Do you expect us to get up and answer the door ourselves?" Gouda bawled down the stairs.

It was the dressmaker with more lace.

"Cinderella, the door!"

It was the milliner with new hats.

"Cinderella, the door!"

It was the dancing master to teach the stepsisters the latest dances in time for the royal ball.

"Cinderella, the door!"

It was the coach, come to take Gouda and Gorgonzola
and their stepfather to the royal palace. The door closed
one last time, and the house fell silent. Cinderella sat down,
put her face in her hands and cried and cried as if her heart
would break.

"So you wanted to go too, did you?"

Cinderella turned round with a start and the sewing box
slipped out of her lap, spilling its contents across the
kitchen floor. She was a little afraid to think that a stranger
– an old beggarwoman – had found her way into the house
uninvited.

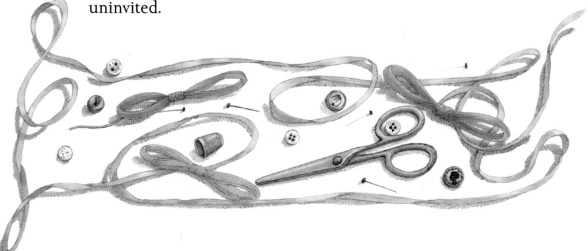

The old woman threw off her ragged cloak. Underneath
she was clothed in a dress of silver gossamer glittering with
dew. This was no beggar. "But, Cinderella, you were entitled
to go. The king invited every unmarried lady of noble birth
to the ball."

"Ah yes, but I don't really count as a lady any more.
Anyway, how did you know who I was . . .?"

"Oh, but I do, Cinderella. I know everything about you:
your goodness and patience and all your heart's desires.
You see, I am your fairy godmother, and I am here to make
sure that your dreams come true."

Then visitors began to arrive for Cinderella: not hairdressers or jewellers or dressmakers, but *fairies*! Yes, fairies from the Land of Dewfall. One brought her a spray of flowers bright as spring. One brought her lizards green as summer. One brought her a pumpkin golden as autumn, and one brought her six mice white as winter. Strange presents, but when nobody has ever given you as much as a kind word, even a lizard can seem a marvellous gift.

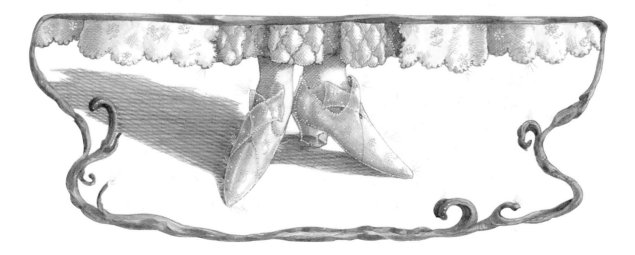

Then her fairy godmother touched each present with a magic wand, and all at once the mice were turned into prancing horses, the pumpkin into a coach of coppery splendour, the lizards into coachmen. "You *shall* go to the royal ball, Cinderella," said her fairy godmother.

"Oh, but will they let me in? Don't you think it would be a rudeness to the prince if I went in these rags?"

Her godmother laughed, and touched the spray of spring blossoms with her wand. Then all at once Cinderella found herself dressed in cream silk and silver satin, a diamond tiara and snowy gloves. And on her tiny feet was a pair of glass slippers.

"Listen hard and listen well, Godchild," said her godmother sternly. "My magic cannot hold past midnight. When the clock strikes twelve, everything will turn back into what it was."

Midnight. It seemed a lifetime away. Ahead lay the whole evening, a magical evening. The Fairies of the Four Seasons fanned her burning cheeks with their wings, and the night sky seemed to be full of stars, all swooping low to gaze at Cinderella's loveliness and to escort her on her way.

Of course she was late. Her stepsisters and father had long since arrived, and the dancing had begun. A fanfare of trumpets announced the prince, and all eyes turned to see the plush scarlet tunic, the dashing run down the grand stairway, the circlet of gold crowning the royal head. As each lady saw him her heart beat faster and her fan fluttered with excitement.

But who could this be now? The trumpets were announcing a latecomer. What bad manners to arrive after the prince!

At the head of the staircase stood a princess – yes, a princess surely! The room caught its breath. The dance music faltered to a silence.

"Who *is* she?"

". . . must come from far away . . ."

". . . a foreign princess . . ."

". . . or we would have heard tell before now of such a beauty!"

The prince looked back up the stairs and his hand rose to his heart. He sprang back up the steps. Fumblingly he pulled off his glove so that he might take her hand and kiss it. But the 'princess' only looked at him with large, round eyes as blue as the summer sea and clasped her hands tightly behind her back. "Would . . . I mean, shall I . . . may I escort you to meet the king?" he said.

"Oh, couldn't we dance first?" whispered Cinderella, not realising that she was speaking to the prince. "I'm terrified of meeting the king or the prince, but you have such a kind, good face: I'm sure I should get up my courage if you would just dance one dance with me." The prince, who had never been asked to dance before, laughed with delight, and escorted her to the dance floor where he swept her round in the dizzying whirl of music.

No wonder the time went fast. The one dance she had asked for turned into two and then into twenty and still the kind young man did not put her to the agony of meeting the king or the prince. When she was thirsty, he brought her oranges. "The rarest fruit in my . . . in the kingdom," he explained. Cinderella took them and sat down beside her father and stepsisters, and split the golden skins and pulled apart the golden segments, sharing them equally.

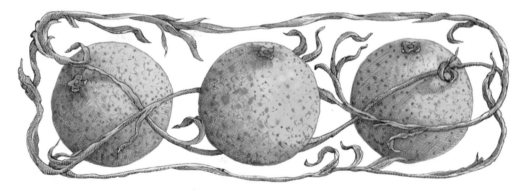

Gouda and Gorgonzola were so busy gazing at the outlandish fruit in their hands, greedily crushing out the juice with curling tongues, that they did not even look the 'princess' in the face. (Besides, loveliness made them jealous.)

One by one the dancers drifted away to other rooms, to the banqueting table, to the balcony and gardens. They could see perfectly well that the prince wanted to be alone with the beautiful stranger. Of course the ugly stepsisters were the last to go: they never noticed anything to do with other people.

"You're so beautiful," said the prince at last.

"Oh, my dress you mean? Yes, isn't it the most wonderful dress you ever saw? My . . . someone gave it to me. Have you seen the shoes? I bet you never saw glass shoes before!"

"I never did," he admitted, laughing. Then realising she still did not know who he was, he went on, "This is foolish. We've danced together all evening and I don't even know your name."

"I –" What could she say? "They call me –" How could she say 'Cinderella' – scullery maid? Little Miss Nobody, who warmed her feet in the ashes?

"I'm sorry, I've kept you to myself all evening," he said (though he did not sound very apologetic), "but I had to be sure."

"Oh, it's been wonderful!" she cried, touching the buttons on his jacket one by one. "Sure of what?"

"Sure I had made the right choice. You know, I suppose, that I love you?"

"Oh no! You can't . . .!"

"Why? You're not in love with someone else, are you?"

"No! But you can't possibly love me . . . at least, not as much as I love you." The prince's face broke into a smile. He had hardly dared to hope the evening would bring him such an exquisite princess. "But there's something I really ought to tell you . . ."

DONG! DONG! went
the great clock bell.
DONG! DONG!
Midnight!

"I must go! I have
to go! I can't stay!
I'm sorry! I'm sorry!"
She broke away from
the prince, as though
to stay another
moment would cost
her her life. She fled
up the staircase.
DONG! DONG! The
clock kept on striking.

Cinderella ran out into the night air and a shock of cold like
icewater. *DONG! DONG!*

"Come back!" cried the prince. "My dear, dearest whoever-
you-are . . . I don't know who you are!" he gasped, and tried
to run after her. But Gouda and Gorgonzola, hoping to
dazzle him with their own beauty, stepped in front of him
and barred his way. *DONG! DONG!* He dodged this way and
that, while they tittered and giggled and curtsied and
fluttered their eyelids.

"Come back! I love you!" called the prince. But Cinderella
did not even look round. She ran on as if wolves were
chasing her – so fast that she stumbled and fell down the
palace steps of white marble. Rolling over and over she
landed – bump – against the wheels of her coppery coach.
She clambered inside and the six white horses sprang
instantly into a gallop. *DONG! DONG!*

The reins went slack. The doors of the coach fell outwards and the wheels rolled away in four separate directions. The coach lizards fell on Cinderella's head, and there she sat on the muddy road, in a hand-me-down dress and one glass shoe.

One shoe? Why should her glass slipper have kept its magic after midnight? And where was the other one?

Cinderella took off the one remaining slipper and put it in her pocket before running home barefoot.

The prince, too, ran out into the cold darkness, still calling, still begging his mysterious dance partner to come back to him. When he could see no trace of her, he put his head in his hands and turned back towards the lights and music.

But wait a minute! What was that, glittering on the steps like a fallen sliver of moon? A glass slipper – so tiny that it might have

belonged to a child. "It's hers! She showed me! I must find her! I must!" And though his guests and his family and his courtiers tried to reason with him the prince was adamant. "Whomsoever the shoe fits, I shall marry. Carry it through the land on a crimson cushion, to every house and home. If Fate decrees we shall marry, the shoe will find its owner, my heart will find its one desire, and I shall find my bride!"

What a stir that caused! The glass slipper carried from door to door, tried on by every lady in the land. And a royal crown for the girl whose foot fitted the tiny slipper. What a temptation! Women were quite ready to crush and crumple their feet into the little shoe, whatever pain it cost them. Gouda and Gorgonzola were quite sure they could do it,

if only they soaked their feet in vinegar, put butter on their heels and rammed home their toes hard and deep enough. The whole house was full of their shrieks and impatience as they awaited the arrival of the prince's pageboy.

"*Cinderella! The DOOR!!!*" they screamed, peering out of the window at the boy bearing the crimson cushion.

"This is our greatest hour! This is what we've always deserved! This is our shining day!"

"But you aren't the pretty girl the prince danced with," said their father, bewildered. "We met her. She sat with us and gave us pieces of orange."

"What's *that* got to do with anything?" demanded Gorgonzola. "He'll never know the difference. Besides, he's said he'll marry 'whomsoever the shoe fits'. So that's his bad luck, isn't it? He shouldn't make such rash promises. Cinderella! Get out of sight, immediately. You make the place look untidy."

So Cinderella slipped out of sight. Her hand, too, slipped out of sight – into the apron pocket where she kept the other glass slipper, that treasured souvenir of her happiest night. She would not be allowed to try on the slipper, of course. But then what would the prince think, anyway, if he knew that his dancing partner was nothing but a scullery maid? A prince! If only she had known. If only he were someone less grand, someone she might have lived in hope of meeting again.

Gouda grabbed the slipper off its cushion and crammed it onto her foot. But you could no more fit a cat into a mousehole.

Gorgonzola snatched it away from her. "Don't be ridiculous, woman. Who'd ever mistake *you* for a mysterious princess? You know it was me, all along. Didn't I sit down beside you, feeding you pieces of orange?" She began to wriggle her foot into the glass slipper. But you could no more fit a horse into a kennel. She and Gouda came to blows, fighting over the shoe, while the page tried to snatch it back and continue his endless, fruitless search.

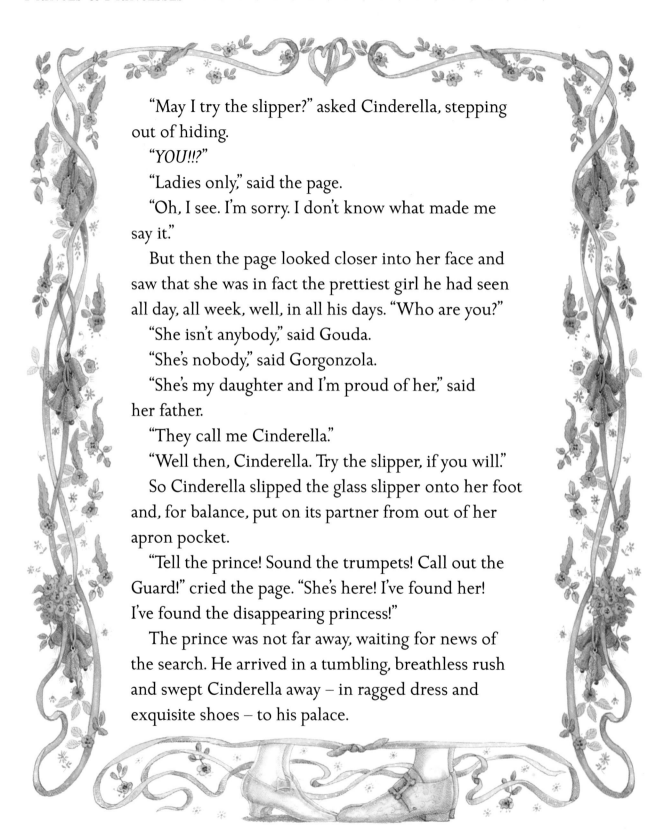

"May I try the slipper?" asked Cinderella, stepping out of hiding.

"*YOU!!?*"

"Ladies only," said the page.

"Oh, I see. I'm sorry. I don't know what made me say it."

But then the page looked closer into her face and saw that she was in fact the prettiest girl he had seen all day, all week, well, in all his days. "Who are you?"

"She isn't anybody," said Gouda.

"She's nobody," said Gorgonzola.

"She's my daughter and I'm proud of her," said her father.

"They call me Cinderella."

"Well then, Cinderella. Try the slipper, if you will."

So Cinderella slipped the glass slipper onto her foot and, for balance, put on its partner from out of her apron pocket.

"Tell the prince! Sound the trumpets! Call out the Guard!" cried the page. "She's here! I've found her! I've found the disappearing princess!"

The prince was not far away, waiting for news of the search. He arrived in a tumbling, breathless rush and swept Cinderella away – in ragged dress and exquisite shoes – to his palace.

And there he married her. And because Cinderella had more sweetness of nature and goodness than either of her sisters she prepared rooms for them inside the royal palace and even found them two courtiers who would love them despite their faults. For, being so happy, she had happiness to spare; it overflowed and filled the land from the dawn in the east to the sunset in the west. It filled the life of her dear prince, too.

THE MAGIC BEAR AND THE HANDSOME PRINCE

Saviour Pirotta

Emma Chichester Clark

A POOR WOMAN HAD TWO ROSE TREES growing outside her cottage, one with beautiful white blooms and the other with red. She also had twin girls, which she had named after the rose trees. Both girls were happy and beautiful but, like the rose trees, they were quite different from each other. Rose Red liked nothing better than to run wild in the meadows, picking flowers and chasing butterflies. Snow White, on the other hand, preferred to stay at home, reading or helping her mother with the household chores.

Every night, after the supper dishes had been washed, the girls would listen to their mother reading a story. They would sit on little cushions and work at their embroidery, while Rose Red's pet dove preened itself on a perch and Snow White's pet lamb snuggled close to the fire.

One winter's night, while Mother was halfway through a fairy tale, there was a loud knock at the door and someone shouted, "Is anyone in?"

"Open up, children," said the mother. "It might be a lost traveller looking for shelter."

Rose Red opened the door, and an enormous brown bear stuck his snout inside the warm cottage. Rose Red screamed and leapt back, while Snow White dived under the table. The lamb bleated in alarm and the dove put its head under a wing.

"Don't be afraid of me," said the bear. "I mean you no harm. It's freezing out here and I just want to warm my paws by the fire."

"Rose Red, let Mr Bear in," said Mother. "Snow White, come out from under that table."

So the bear came in and sat by the fire. Mother continued the story and pretty soon, the girls grew bold and leant against the bear for comfort. The lamb too came close and snuggled up to him, while the dove pulled its head out from under its wing and went on preening its feathers.

At the end of the story, the bear asked the girls to brush his coat. They fetched a broom and swept his back until his fur was sleek and smooth. Then they went to bed, while their new friend stretched out and went to sleep by the fire.

In the morning, the girls let the bear out and he wandered off into the snow. But that evening he returned to hear more stories and to sleep at the hearth. And so it continued till the spring came and the snow in the forest began to melt. Then the bear said, "I shall not return tonight. I must go to the mountains where I have to guard my treasure from the dwarves. In winter, when the ground is frozen, they cannot dig it up, but in spring, when the ground is soft, they manage to dig through and steal my gold."

Snow White and Rose Red were quite sad when they heard that the bear would not be visiting any longer, for they had grown very fond of him. Snow White opened the door, and as the bear passed through, the bolt snagged him on the hip and pulled off a chunk of his soft fur. Rose Red thought she saw a flash of gold underneath but she wasn't sure, and she did not say anything about it. The bear ran off across the snow and was soon lost to sight.

A few days later, Snow White and Rose Red went into the forest to collect some firewood. There they found a fallen tree lying across the path. Behind it, something was jumping up and down like a giant grasshopper. When they got nearer, they saw it was a dwarf with his long beard trapped under the tree trunk.

"How did you manage to get trapped so, good sir?" asked Rose Red.

"If you must know, you meddling creatures, I was chopping some wood to cook my dinner," snarled the dwarf. "There's nothing wrong with that, is there?

Now come on, don't just stand there, help me pull my
beard out."

The girls tugged at the beard with all their strength,
but it was no use; the poor dwarf seemed well and truly
stuck. So Snow White whipped out a pair of scissors
and – snip, snip – she cut off the tip of his beard.

"What did you do that for?" screamed the dwarf.
"How can I go about with the tip of my beard missing?
You silly, insolent creatures, don't meddle with me or
I'll put a curse on you." And without as much as a 'thank
you for freeing me', he pulled a bag of gold out of the
hollow tree trunk and disappeared with it into the forest.

The girls hoped they would never run into the
ungrateful dwarf again but barely a week had passed
when they met him once more by a brook. The girls
had gone there to catch a fish for their supper and,
as they approached the water, they saw something
leaping about in the reeds. At first they thought it was
a giant frog, then, as they got closer, they realised it
was the rude dwarf.

"Good morning," said Rose Red. "And what is the
matter with you today?"

"Can't you see?" snapped the dwarf. "My blessed beard
has got tangled in my fishing line and a big fish is about
to pull me into the water. Help me, will you? Don't just
stand there, watching me drown."

The girls tried very hard to disentangle the dwarf
from the tackle but the fish kept pulling the line out
of their hands. So, once again, Snow White produced
her sewing scissors and – snip, snip – she cut off a good
portion of the dwarf's beard.

"Are you mad?" howled the dwarf the moment he was free. "Can't you see that you have disfigured my face completely? I'll never be able to show my face outside the house again. But I'll pay you back, you insolent hussies, never fear." And with that, he fished a bag of pearls out from among the reeds and disappeared down the road.

A week later, the girl's mother sent them to buy ribbons at the market. Their way lay across the heath and, as they walked past a huge rock, they saw an enormous eagle wheeling overhead. The eagle landed behind the rock and a moment later the girls heard someone howling in agony. They ran round the rock, and what did they find? The eagle had snatched their old friend the dwarf by the seat of his trousers and was trying to lift him off the ground.

"Get over here and help me, will you?" cried the dwarf. "Can't you see this monster is about to have me for its breakfast?"

At once, the girls grabbed the dwarf by his coat-tails and tried to pull him free from the eagle's claws. The eagle pulled too, but its claws were no match for the strong girls. At last it let go of the dwarf and flew off into the sky.

"You clumsy creatures," said the dwarf to the girls as he rubbed his bottom. "Couldn't you have been a bit more careful with my coat? Look, it's torn to shreds. Now I'll have to spend money on another one." Then he prised a bag of diamonds out from under the rock and was gone.

On their way home from the market, the girls chanced upon the dwarf a fourth time. He was sitting on the grass, with his diamonds scattered in piles around him. The evening sun shone on the precious stones and made them shimmer and sparkle. The girls, who had never seen a precious stone close up before, couldn't help staring.

"What are you gawping at?" shouted the dwarf, who had not been expecting anyone out on the heath so late. "Have you never seen diamonds before, or are you planning to kill me and rob me? Be off with you, you vandals, you robbers, you thieves—" He was still raging and howling when a bear leapt out of the trees and pounced on him. The dwarf's attitude changed right away.

"Please, dear bear," he begged, "do not harm me. I'll give you all my treasure. Eat those girls instead of me. They're much bigger than I am and their flesh is not so tough."

But the bear ignored his pleas; he raised his enormous paw and – thwack – dealt him a mighty blow. The dwarf fell limp on the ground.

The girls screamed and started running away. But the bear called out to them and said, "Snow White, Rose Red, wait for me."

Then the girls recognised their old friend and stopped running. They waited for him to catch up with them and, as he approached, his fur melted away and he was transformed into a handsome prince.

"I am a king's son," he said. "That wicked dwarf stole my treasure and put a spell on me, so that I was forced to live as a bear until he was slain. Now I am free to go home."

Some time later Snow White married the prince and
Rose Red his brother. The girls' mother came to live with
them in the palace and she brought her two rose trees with
her. Every year they continued to bear the most beautiful
blooms: snow white and rose red.

The
Prince AND THE
Flying Carpet

Margaret Mayo

Jane Ray

THERE WAS ONCE A PRINCE who was so fond of hunting that he rode out every day in search of game. But one day he had no luck and by late afternoon had caught nothing. He rode on and on until he reached a dark jungle where he had never been before. There he came upon a flock of parrots, perched in amongst the trees, and he lifted his bow and took aim.

But before he could shoot, there was a whirl and flurry of feathers and the parrots flew up and away, leaving one bird still sitting there.

"Do not shoot me!" said the bird. "I am the raja of all parrots. I am the one that can tell you about Princess Maya."

The prince lowered his bow and rode up to the bird. "Princess Maya!" he said. "Who is Princess Maya?"

"Ahhh – the beautiful Princess Maya," said the parrot. "What can I say? She is radiant as the moon . . . warm and gentle as the evening sun. In this great world she is beyond compare."

"Where does she live?" asked the prince. "And how can I find her?"

"Go forward, ever forward," said the parrot, "through dark jungles and across wide plains, and you will find her."

Then the prince rode home and on the way he made up his mind to find the beautiful Princess Maya, even if he had to search the whole world.

When he told his mother and father about the beautiful princess, they were sad. He was their only child, their golden treasure, and they did not want to lose him. But the prince had decided to go and he would not change his mind.

The very next morning he dressed in his finest clothes, took his bow and arrows and some food for the journey, mounted his favourite horse and set off.

Well, he rode until he reached the dark jungle where he
had seen the parrots. And then he rode forward, ever
forward. He crossed a wide plain, and still he rode forward.
He entered a second, even darker, jungle and, all of a sudden,
he heard loud, angry voices; and in a clearing near by, he
saw three demons – three small, sharp-eyed, wicked-looking
demons – bunched round a small pile of things lying on the
ground. There was a bag, a stick and an ancient carpet.

"What is the matter?" asked the prince.

One of the demons pointed to the things lying on the
ground. "Our master died and left us these," he said, "and I
want *all* of them!"

"And so do I!" shouted the second demon.

"Me too!" shrieked the third.

"A bag, a stick and an old carpet?" said the prince. "They're
not worth quarrelling about!"

"Not worth quarrelling about!" The first demon squalled
it out, fair cracked his throat. "Not worth quarrelling about!
Why, the bag will give you anything you ask for. And the
stick will beat your enemies and – see the rope coiled
round it? – that will tie them up so they can't escape. As for
the carpet . . . it will take you anywhere you want to go."

"Is that so?" said the prince. And he did some quick thinking. "Maybe I could help settle the quarrel," he suggested. "I shall take three arrows and shoot them in the air, and the first one of you to find an arrow and bring it back can have all the treasures."

"Yes! Yes!" the little demons agreed. Each one certain *he* was the fastest runner. Each one certain *he* would win.

So the prince let fly three arrows, and off they ran, full pelt.

And what next? The prince jumped down from his horse, turned it round to face the way they had come and said, "Lift your hooves, my fine horse, and gallop home!" And the horse galloped off.

The prince picked up the stick and the bag. He unrolled the carpet, sat down on it, crossed his legs and said, "Carpet! Take me to the city where Princess Maya lives!"

The carpet fluttered and then rose slowly upwards.
When it was higher than the trees, it simply flew through
the air. Smooth and steady, it flew and flew, over dark
jungles and wide plains. It flew and it flew, until it came to
the edge of a great city. Then it gently floated downwards.

As soon as the carpet touched the ground, the prince
stood up, stretched himself and looked around. He rolled
up the carpet and, with the bag over his shoulder, the carpet
tucked under his arm and the stick in his hand, he strode
off into the city.

The first person he met was an old woman. "Is this the
city where Princess Maya lives?" he asked.

"Indeed it is," she said.

"And how can I find her?" he asked.

"Every evening," said the woman, "the princess comes and
sits upon the palace roof for one whole hour, and – *Oh! Such
great wonder!* – she lights the city with her beauty."

So that evening the prince waited outside the palace, and
at sunset a slender maiden came and sat upon the roof. She
wore a sari of shimmering silk and on her forehead was a
golden band, set with diamonds and pearls. It seemed as if

a silvery radiance shone around her: in her presence night
became day.

The prince gazed upon the beautiful Princess Maya.
He could not take his eyes off her. She truly was beyond
compare.

At midnight he held his bag and he said, "Bag! Give me
a shawl of shimmering silk, the very match of Princess
Maya's sari!" And there – inside the bag – was a shawl of
shimmering silk.

He unrolled his carpet, sat down, crossed his legs and
said, "Carpet! Take me to Princess Maya!"

The carpet rose up until it was higher than the roofs and
flew over the city until it reached the palace. Then it went
straight through an open window and landed in Princess
Maya's room.

The prince looked around and saw the beautiful princess,
lying asleep in her bed.

Soft and silent as a cat, he stood up and gently placed the
silk shawl beside the sleeping princess. And then – back on
the carpet – he was off!

The next evening the prince again stood outside the
palace and gazed upon the beautiful princess; and at
midnight he said, "Bag! Give me a necklace of diamonds and
pearls, the very match of Princess Maya's golden headband!"
And there it was – a golden necklace set with diamonds
and pearls.

Again he unrolled his carpet, sat down, crossed his legs
and said, "Carpet! Take me to Princess Maya!" And again off
he flew, right into her room. And this time he placed the
necklace beside the sleeping princess. Then – back on the
carpet – he was off!

On the third evening the same things happened. The prince stood outside and gazed upon the beautiful princess; and at midnight he said, "Bag! Give me a golden ring set with the finest diamonds in the world!" And there it was – a splendid glittering ring.

Again he unrolled his carpet, sat down, crossed his legs and flew to the palace and into her room.

But his time he did not place the gift beside the sleeping princess. Instead he lifted her hand and slipped the ring on one of her fingers.

Princess Maya stirred and opened her eyes. And when she saw the handsome young prince who held her hand, she said, "So, you are the one who gave me the shawl and the necklace and now this ring. Tell me, is there something you want, something I can give you in return?"

"There is," said the prince. "You yourself are the gift I seek, for you are the one I wish to marry."

Princess Maya was surprised by the prince's words, but after they had talked together for much of the night she agreed to marry this handsome, generous young man. And in the morning she took him to her father, the raja of that land, and asked for his consent to their marriage.

But the raja said, "This man is a stranger. One who came like a thief in the night. You cannot marry him."

The princess pleaded with her father until at last he agreed that if the prince could prove that he was a man of courage and strength then she could marry him.

The raja said to the prince, "Outside the city there lives a fearsome ogre. He is as tall as two, as broad as three and has the strength of six. My people live in fear of him. Day in, day out, he comes and kills and steals. If you can

capture this ogre, then you may marry my daughter."

The prince thought to himself, "Capture an ogre? *This is a task I can surely do!*" And he set off with the stick in his hand.

He had not gone far when the mighty ogre saw him and came bounding towards him, roaring and bellowing in a great fury.

The prince said, "Stick! Do your work!" And the stick went flying through the air, and it beat the ogre until he fell helpless to the ground.

Then the prince said, "Rope! Do your work!" And the rope twirled itself off the stick and, quick as lightning, coiled itself round the ogre until he was bound, head to toe, so tight that he couldn't even move his little finger.

What then could the raja say? He had to agree to the marriage of the prince and his beautiful daughter, Princess Maya. So there was a wedding. And such a wedding! For a whole week there was feasting and rejoicing throughout the land.

At last the time came for the prince to return to his
own land with his new bride. Then there was a long and
magnificent procession: the prince and princess and their
attendants led the way, riding splendid black horses, and
behind them trooped a hundred camels, bells jingling,
all laden with treasures the raja had heaped upon them.

Now when the prince's horse had returned to the royal
stables without a rider, his mother and father had been
certain that their son was dead. So – imagine their happiness
when he returned with his beautiful bride!

Well, the years passed, and the prince and beautiful
Princess Maya lived together, happy and content. The prince
always kept the bag, the stick and the carpet with him. And
while the bag and the carpet were often useful, because his
was a peaceful country and he had no enemies, he never
again needed to use the stick.

BEAUTY AND THE BEAST

ROSE IMPEY

IAN BECK

THERE ONCE WAS A MAN who set out on a journey full of hope, but returned in complete despair. Only a year earlier this man had been a rich and respected merchant in the city, but unexpectedly he had lost everything and been forced to move with his family to a small cottage in the country, and there life was hard.

But now word had arrived that a ship had landed carrying valuable cargo that belonged to him, and his family had high hopes of soon returning to their old life. The man said goodbye to his three sons and three daughters, taking with him lists of presents they had begged him to bring back. All except his youngest daughter, Beauty. She was so called because of her lovely face and her sweet nature.

"And what would you like, Beauty?" he asked his favourite child.

"Only your safe return, Father," she said. But when Beauty saw the scornful look her two sisters gave her, she added, "Perhaps you could bring me a rose. There are so few growing in these parts."

And the man set off, never realising how dear that present would cost him.

When he finally reached the port the man found that the whole cargo had already been sold and used to pay off old debts; there wasn't a penny left. He turned homewards, weighed down with the disappointment he knew his children would feel, and this made his journey seem longer.

He was still thirty miles from home when he lost his way in a forest. A storm blew up, so severe that it more than once

threatened to throw him off his horse. He began to search
for shelter. He feared that by morning he'd either be frozen
to death or eaten by wolves. He could hear them howling
close by.

The man saw a flickering light through the trees, and
following it came at last to a very grand house. Normally
he would never have dared to approach such a place. But his
horse, of its own accord, went into the stables and began to
eat hay and oats from a manger. The man headed towards
the house.

Although he knocked several times no one came to
answer, so the man pushed open the door and entered the
hall. There he found a good fire and a table set with silver
and crystal and laid with food for one person. He stood
before the fire to dry out his clothes, expecting the owner
or a servant to appear, but no one came. The house
remained silent, apparently deserted.

By eleven o'clock the man couldn't control his hunger and,
in desperation, sat down and ate the meal that was waiting
there. When he'd finished he set out to discover whose
house it was. He passed through many beautiful rooms,

high-ceilinged and richly furnished, but he met no one and found no sign of life.

Eventually he came to a small bedroom. The bed was ready-made and warmed, as if a visitor was expected. The man was so tired that he lay down between the soft white sheets and fell asleep. It was past ten in the morning when he woke, completely rested. His adventure the night before now seemed nothing more than a bad dream. Beside his bed he found a set of new clothes and as he dressed the man wondered what kind of spirit it was that was looking after him so well.

When he looked out of his bedroom window the man was surprised to see no evidence of last night's storm, only a perfectly tranquil garden. He went back to the hall and found breakfast waiting for him. He sat down and ate. When he had finished he said out loud, "I'm truly grateful for the hospitality you've shown me, but now I think it's time for me to leave."

Even then no one came near, so the man went in search of his horse. His way to the stables led him through a rose garden and the man suddenly remembered his daughter's request. Sadly he realised that this would be the only present he would manage to take back. He chose the loveliest rose and broke off a single stem.

Instantly there was a terrifying howl. Coming towards him the man saw a dreadful figure, a beast, so hideously ugly that it was almost enough to make him faint.

"You ungrateful wretch! How dare you?" roared the beast. "After I have saved your life, this is the thanks you show me, to steal the thing I prize above all else. Well, you will die for this."

The man was almost paralysed by fear but he fell on his knees and begged the beast's forgiveness.

"My lord, do not be angry with me. A flower seemed such a trifle, compared with what you have already done for me. I would never have taken it for myself; it was to fulfil a promise I made to one of my daughters."

"I am no lord – my name is Beast," he snarled. "Don't waste your flattery on me; I despise compliments. Neither am I interested in your excuses. However, since you say you have daughters, I will spare you – if one of them is willing to suffer in your place."

This was no comfort to the man.

"How could I persuade a child whom I love to die for me?" he asked.

"I never spoke of persuasion," said the beast. "She must come willingly, or not at all. You are now free to leave, but within three months either you or one of your daughters must return. Give me your word on it."

The man offered no argument; he gave the beast his word.

There was no question of sending one of his daughters in his place but at least this way he would be allowed to say goodbye to them all before he died.

"You will not return home penniless," said the beast. "In your room is a chest. Fill it with whatever you like and I will send it on to you. But do not think to break your promise," he warned. Then the beast was gone; the man was alone once more.

"Well," he thought, "I must be grateful that my family won't be left poor when I die." He filled the chest with gold pieces, locked it, and went on his way in the deepest despair.

His horse seemed to find its own route and, sooner than he expected, the man reached home, where his family was anxiously waiting for him. Despite their disappointment to see him empty-handed, they were relieved to have him home safe.

When he gave Beauty the rose he'd brought her, the man burst into tears.

"If you had only known how much this rose would cost me, Beauty," he said. And when they'd heard his story Beauty's sisters wept too. They turned on her angrily.

"You're to blame for this. Always trying to be better

than us! Now our father will die and all because of you. Yet you stand there calmly, as if you didn't care."

"Why shouldn't I be calm?" asked Beauty. "There's no need for our father to die, because I intend to go in his place. I'd never let him suffer on my account."

Then there was much argument between them.

"No, Beauty, we'll go instead," insisted her brothers. "We'll fight the beast or die in the attempt."

"There's no point," said their father. "The beast's far too powerful for us. Anyway, I gave him my word. No, I'm the one to go. After all, my life's nearly over."

But Beauty said, "Father, I won't let you die. My mind's made up. Don't try to persuade me. I shall only follow you." And she persisted until she had convinced them. Her jealous sisters needed no convincing. They were delighted at the thought of getting rid of her. They couldn't have planned it better themselves.

When the man went to bed that night he was surprised to find the chest of gold in his bedroom. He told Beauty his secret because he trusted her, but decided not to tell his other children. He knew that they would want to return to the city, and he'd made up his mind to stay in the country from now on. However, Beauty persuaded her father to share the gold. While the old man had been away her sisters had been courted by two gentlemen, and the gold would allow them to make good marriages.

But it seemed as if the more love and kindness she showed her sisters the more they resented her. When the time came for Beauty's father to take her to the beast, the only way the heartless pair could show any sadness at losing her was by rubbing their eyes with an onion.

All too soon Beauty and her father reached the beast's
house. Again the horse made its own way into the stable.
When they entered the hall a meal was waiting for them,
and despite her own fear Beauty coaxed her father to eat
a little.

Without warning, a dreadful noise started up, a kind of
deep growling, and there was the beast beside them. Beauty's
father began to tremble and, when she saw the beast for the
first time, so did Beauty; he was even uglier than she'd
expected. But when he spoke to her in his terrifying voice,
she answered as bravely as she could.

"Well, Beauty, have you come willingly?" he asked.

"Yes," she whispered.

"Good," said the beast. "I'm glad to see you have kept your
word, old man. In the morning you must leave and never
think to return. Goodbye, for now, Beauty." And the beast
went as suddenly as he had come. He left Beauty and her
father in a state of terror.

"Oh, my dear, how could I even think of letting you stay here?" said her father. "You must go home and I will remain."

But Beauty was feeling calmer by now. "Don't worry, Father, I'm not afraid. I shall trust fate to take care of me. Let's make good use of the time we have left together. Tomorrow will come soon enough."

At bedtime neither of them expected to rest easily, but the moment their heads touched their pillows they were asleep. Beauty dreamed about a fine lady who said to her, "You have shown great courage in sacrificing yourself for your father. Don't be afraid, your goodness will not go unrewarded."

In the morning Beauty told her father about her dream. It gave them each some comfort, but when it came time for them to part her father wept bitterly.

After he'd left, Beauty wept too, but at length she convinced herself that it served no purpose. If she had only a little time to live then surely she should make the best of it. The house and gardens were very beautiful and she decided to explore them.

She came to a door on which were the words 'Beauty's Room'. Inside was everything she could have wished for: books without number, musical instruments and plenty of music to play.

She began to think, "If I had only the rest of the day to live, why would such trouble have been taken to please me? Perhaps the beast doesn't intend to kill me so soon." Feeling more hopeful she picked up a book and opened it. Inside was an inscription:

Welcome, Beauty, do not fear,
You are queen and mistress here.
Whether it be night or day,
Only speak and we'll obey.

"There's nothing else I want," she said aloud, "except to see my poor father, and I know you can't grant that." But even as she spoke she caught sight of the looking glass on the wall. In it she could see moving images: her father arriving home, sad and dejected, her sisters, pretending to be sorry, yet clearly pleased to be rid of her. The next moment the mirror cleared and the picture was gone. But it had given Beauty some comfort and further evidence of the beast's kindness towards her.

There was food set out for her at midday. While she ate, music played, although she saw no sign of human life. But in the evening, as she was dining, the beast appeared; the same dreadful noises warned of his approach.

"Beauty, may I sit beside you while you eat?" he asked.

Beauty hardly dared to answer. "You are master here."

"Oh no," said the beast, "you are mistress now. I will try

to do whatever you wish. But tell me the truth, do you find me hideously ugly?"

Although Beauty hesitated she couldn't bring herself to lie. "You may be ugly, but you've been kind to me and I'm grateful for that."

"Oh, I can be kind," said the beast, "yet I am still ugly and stupid and unworthy of you. Am I not completely repulsive?"

"No, you're not," said Beauty honestly. "Many people who look handsome have an ugly soul or a cruel heart. It's more important what a person is inside than what he appears outside."

Encouraged by these words the beast suddenly surprised her by asking, "Beauty, will you marry me?"

Beauty's heart began to beat fast. She was afraid of refusing the beast, but she couldn't bear the thought of marrying him.

"No, Beast, I won't," she said bravely.

The beast roared angrily and leaped to his feet and Beauty thought that even now he might kill her. But he left her and she didn't see him again that day.

During the three months that Beauty remained with the beast she never saw another human being. At mealtimes food was always waiting for her, and unseen hands provided everything she might need. Every evening the beast joined her while she ate. Rather than dread his visits, she came to look forward to his company. He had little conversation, but he was thoughtful and what he had to say interested her. But each night before he left he caused her the same pain and fear when he asked, "Beauty, will you marry me?"

Every time he asked she refused him. "It would be dishonest to pretend that I might change my mind. I've come to care for you as a friend, and I wouldn't hurt you, but I can't marry you."

"Then promise never to leave me. I feel as if I would die if we were parted," said the beast.

Beauty could have made this promise easily, but each day she looked into the mirror and watched her father becoming weaker with worrying about her.

"I would happily stay with you if only I could see my father. Now that my sisters are married and my brothers have left to join the army he's all alone. I know he misses me and it breaks my heart."

"Then go back to him," said the beast. "I'll die here without you, but I would rather that than have you suffer."

"I don't want to be the cause of your death," said Beauty. "Let me visit my father for one week and then I'll come back and stay with you for ever."

The beast gave Beauty a ring. "As soon as you are ready to come home, place this ring beside your bed. Goodbye, Beauty, and remember – without you I shall certainly die." With these words in her mind Beauty went to bed, deeply troubled.

When she woke, Beauty found herself in her old bedroom at home. She went to look for her father, and for the next two hours they sat talking together, unwilling to be parted. At last Beauty went to dress. Word had been sent to tell her sisters that she was home and they were expected shortly.

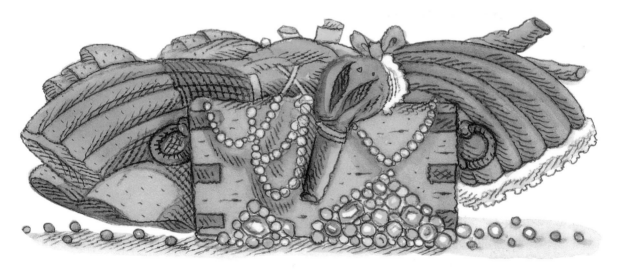

In her bedroom she found a chest containing the most elegant dresses and exquisite jewellery. Beauty began to share them out to give her sisters, but the moment she told her father what she was doing the dresses disappeared.

"I think the beast may have intended the dresses for you," said her father, and the dresses instantly reappeared.

Beauty chose one to wear and hurried to greet her sisters. Having made unhappy marriages, they both looked thoroughly miserable. The eldest had married a handsome but vain man, so full of his own importance that he hardly paid any attention to his wife. The second sister had married a man well-known for his wit and sarcastic tongue, which he used to ridicule everyone around him, especially his wife.

When her sisters saw the wonderful clothes Beauty owned and heard how happy she was living with the beast, they were bitterly jealous.

"How is it that she always does better than we do?" asked the eldest. "What has she ever done to deserve such good fortune?"

"Nothing," agreed the second sister. "Nothing at all. I could scream. I wish the beast *had* eaten her. It would have served her right."

The eldest sister smiled at this.

"If we can persuade her to stay longer than a week," she said, "perhaps the beast will be so angry he really will eat her."

The sisters decided to pretend to be so happy to have Beauty home that she would be unable to leave them for fear of breaking their hearts. They acted their parts so well, showing such love towards her, that Beauty was entirely taken in. When it came time to leave she couldn't bear to upset them and they soon persuaded her to stay. This went on each day until she had been two weeks away from the beast.

However, Beauty felt wretched at having broken her word and she worried daily how the beast was managing without her. One night in a dream she saw the beast lying in his garden, dying of misery. He reproached her, reminding her of her broken promise. Beauty woke up, shivering and crying.

"How could I do such a thing," she asked herself, "when he's treated me with so much kindness? What does it matter if he's ugly? He has a good and generous heart and is far more worthy of love than either of my sisters' husbands. I must go back to him. Even if I cannot love him as a husband, I know that I love him as a friend."

She placed the ring beside her bed and went back to sleep. She was greatly relieved when she woke the next morning to find herself back in the beast's house.

Beauty dressed carefully, wanting to please the beast. Then she occupied herself as best she could until the time came when he was expected to join her. But that time came and passed, and still he didn't appear. Beauty searched first in the house and then the gardens.

She began to feel a dreadful sense of urgency, as if she knew that with each minute that passed her chances of finding him alive were disappearing.

At the point when she felt in complete despair she pictured him as she'd seen him in her dream, and then she knew where to look. Beside the river which flowed along the edge of the garden, she found him lying, almost dead, on a grassy bank.

The sight of him caused her such pain that she dropped to her knees and held him close to her.

"Oh, Beast," she begged, "speak to me. I've treated you so cruelly. Tell me you forgive me."

The beast stirred and gave a weary sigh. "Is that really you, Beauty? Now I can die in peace."

"Don't think of dying," she said. "I've come back and I'll never leave you again. I thought that I loved you only as a friend, but now I can see that I can't live without you. I want to be your wife."

The words were barely spoken before there were strange, echoing sounds in the air around them, a shimmering quality to the light and at the same time a transformation in the beast. These strange happenings lasted hardly a minute and when they were over Beauty found herself looking at a young and handsome man, who lay smiling up at her.

He began to explain, but she would hardly let him speak before she felt compelled to ask, "Where is my beast gone?"

"He's here, before you, trying to tell you how you have saved his life," laughed the young man. "A cruel fairy imprisoned me in the skin of the beast until a time when a good and beautiful woman agreed to be my wife. You have freed me and now I can ask you in my own right: Beauty, will you marry me?"

Once she was certain that this was the same beast she had come to love, albeit in a different form, she gladly accepted.

They returned to the house, where they found Beauty's family waiting for them and also the fine lady whom Beauty recognised from her dream.

"You have done well," she told Beauty. "Your goodness and generous spirit have brought happiness both to yourself and your prince. Your wisdom will make you a good queen. As for your sisters," she said, turning to face them, "until you truly regret your past wickedness, you will stand outside your sister's palace as a pair of statues. There you will be able to see the rewards she has earned and consider how different your own lives might have been."

Then all of them were transported to the prince's own kingdom, where Beauty married the prince and lived happily, just as she deserved.

07775874832

The
FIREBIRD

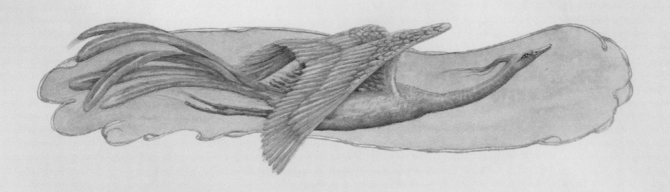

GERALDINE MCCAUGHREAN

ANGELA BARRETT

ONCE, BESIDE THE WALL of an ancient castle, the sun shone down on a clearing amid dense, tall trees. You would have thought it was a garden left to run wild, for here and there stone statues stood overgrown with ivy or sprawled in the long grass. But with a closer look, your blood would have run cold. For they were not statues, but the petrified, stony remains of unhappy travellers. Young men and old there were, pedlars and dukes: anyone unlucky enough to pass by Castle Pitiless and be seen by the wicked Koschei. The castle was the evil sorcerer's lair, and his cruel magic stretched out from its walls in pools of black shadow. No matter where the sun stood in the sky, those shadows stretched to north, south, east and west.

There were no pretty girls among the statues. Koschei preferred simply to take girls prisoner and keep them captive in Castle Pitiless, where he could enjoy looking at them. Like a cat watching goldfish in a pond.

One summer's day yet another young man strayed, unsuspecting, into the pretty wooded glade in Koschei's forest. He was Prince Ivan, separated from his fellow huntsmen and wandering lost among the trees, enjoying the birdsong.

All of a sudden, like fire from a dragon's mouth, a flash of orange streamed past his face. Then it was high above his head; next it was swooping through the long grass. A female bird the colour of flame, with streamers of fiery plumage, soared and tumbled between the branches, delighting in the warm sunshine. Ivan hid behind a tree so as not to scare her away.

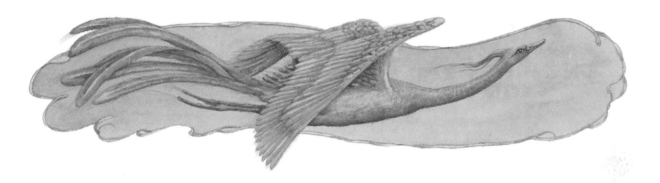

If ever good magic perched in an evil roost it was when the Firebird took her morning flight through the woods of Castle Pitiless. Prince Ivan gazed open-mouthed at her sheer speed and grace as she somersaulted through the sunbeams, filling her cloak of feathers with the gusting wind. Just for a moment she settled on the grass.

"Got you!" cried Prince Ivan, leaping out of his hiding place and wrapping both arms round her. "Wait till my friends see what I've caught on the hunt!" She struggled, but he held on tightly.

"No! No! Let me go! You must!" She twisted and writhed, but he would not free her. "If you have a drop of pity in you, sir, please don't cage me! I'll die if I can't fly in the open sky!"

Her tears alarmed him dreadfully. With one hand he smoothed her tousled plumage and with the other he set her down on her slender claws. "Shush! There, there! Calm yourself. Hush. Do you think I'd really keep hold of you if it meant harming you? I'm sorry. That's how we men are sometimes. When we see real beauty we can't help wanting to grab hold, to own it. I'm sorry to frighten you."

The Firebird trembled from head to foot, darted away to a safe distance, then stood looking at him. "You're a good, kind man. You won't be sorry you let me go. You think I'm weak, but I'm really quite powerful. Here. Have this."

She plucked a scarlet feather from her breast and held it out to him. "If you ever need help, call me with this feather and I shall come in an instant." Then, with a flourish of her extraordinary wings, the Firebird soared into the air like the Pheonix which is born and reborn in a burst of flame.

She was no sooner gone than Prince Ivan heard voices – girls' voices – and another sudden flurry of colour burst

into the clearing. He quickly hid again, to see what new
wonders the wood had to offer.

But the girls who ran by were not like the Firebird. They
were happy enough in their games and their dancing, but
they were not free. Every time they looked back towards the
castle, their faces grew sad. And each time they came across
one of the stone statues, they flinched from it in horror.

One, the tallest, Ivan thought every bit as beautiful as
the Firebird. He could not take his eyes off her. He left his
hiding place just to see her better, and his heart burned
as though the feather inside his jacket was truly a flicker
of fire.

When the girls saw Ivan, they were startled and afraid.
"Please don't run away! I won't hurt you," he said. And
beckoning to one of them, he whispered, "Please won't you
introduce me to that lady there – the one all in blue?"

"Princess Nadeshda, you mean?"

They barely needed an introduction. For the princess was
looking at Ivan much as he had looked at her. There was
magic in that woodland glade, and not all of it was bad.

The love between them was instant – like a lightning strike. But for the second time that day Prince Ivan found he could not take home with him the beauty he admired so much. "We are all prisoners of the evil sorcerer Koschei," explained the princess. "He lets us out of . . . *that place* every day to breathe fresh air, but we can no more leave than if we were chained to the castle keep. This forest is just the pleasantest part of Koschei's prison . . . And you are inside it too, Ivan! Go now, before he sees you. Girls he keeps like castle pets, but men he turns to stone. See the statues? Now go! Forget me. Forget us all. Just go, before Koschei finds you. I couldn't bear it if you were to . . ."

A dismal bell began to toll inside Castle Pitiless, like the clang of a funeral knell. The girls at once began to move away, with slow, sad steps, looking back over their shoulders, powerless to stay. The iron gates in the wall swung shut behind them.

"No! Don't go!" Ivan begged, shaking at the gates with desperate hands. And the gates did indeed swing open again.

But this time it was not pretty girls who came out but demons, goblins, trolls and gremlins, beasts with furry jowls and piggy snouts, some with fangs, more with clawed paws snatching at Ivan's clothes and skin. They swept round him in a black flood, until he was marooned, cut off from all escape.

Then came Koschei – so huge he had to duck his head beneath the tree branches, and broke the mistletoe off the boughs. His long hair and beard were plaited with thorns and his face was the colour of pestilence. "So! Another intruder, eh? Another trespasser! And what do we do with men who come where they're not invited?"

"*Turn them to stone! Turn them to stone!*" chanted his beastly, ferocious henchmen. "Do it, o master, for we love to sharpen our teeth on the Stone Ones and blunt our claws on them!"

"So be it!" cried Koschei. "Let him be turned to . . ."

Ivan did not know whether it was magic or fear that gripped his legs, that stole all the strength out of his arms. He felt an icy chill taking hold of him, of every part but one burning pool above his heart. It took all the strength he could muster to pull out the Firebird's feather and brandish it at Koschei.

"So soon?" came a cry from overhead. "Do you need my help so soon?" Down came the Firebird to stand beside him, her wings furling behind her like folds of a streaming, scarlet cloak.

"Oho! No grey stone death for *you*, my beauty!" laughed Koschei. "I shall put *you* in a cage and hang you in my window to sing for me!"

Then Prince Ivan regretted summoning the Firebird into such danger. For what could she do against so many terrible foes?

"Will you so?" said the Firebird. "And if I sing, will you dance?" Her wings cracked open like the panels of a kite.

All at once Koschei's demons began to shuffle about, then to shamble, with rolling shoulders and waving arms, in a kind of ugly jig. "*Dance*, Koschei!" commanded the Firebird, and even the giant ogre was powerless to disobey. His huge feet began to stamp, then to jump, then to skip crazily about, his big head lolling about on his neck, and his hands shaking themselves loose at the ends of his arms.

He hopped and jigged like a man overjoyed, but his face scowled and he yelled curses as the Firebird's magic forced him to dance on and on. She led the dancing, weaving in and out between the trees.

The goblins and ghouls, gremlins and demons groaned and moaned; their muscles ached, but their limbs would not let them rest. They sprang and vaulted over one another, begging their master to put a stop to their torment. They danced till the fur on their paws wore out. Koschei's shiny slippers flapped and scuffed, and the heels flew off in two different directions.

At last, when they were totally exhausted, the Firebird allowed them to rest. They dropped where they stood, panting and sobbing, and fell into an instant, snoring sleep. All but Koschei. He fell flat on his face, but his eyelids stayed open, watching. The Firebird herself showed not the smallest sign of weariness.

Ivan drew his hunting dagger and ran towards the sorcerer, swearing to kill him and put an end to all his filthy enchantments. The grisly ogre only bared his teeth in a spiteful grin.

"Can't kill me, pipsqueak," he panted. "I keep my soul in a safe place – outside my body – hidden away from fools like you."

Ivan turned to the Firebird for help, but it seemed she had no more magic to lend him. "Search out that soul, Ivan," she said. "Find it and destroy it. All his spells will be broken!" She spread her wings, preparing to leave. "I do remember, when I've flown through this wood before, seeing something round and white in the bole of a rotten tree . . . Goodbye now!"

His hand still raised in farewell, his thanks still echoing among the branches, Ivan started to search, racing from tree to tree. All the trunks looked green and sappy. Just one was black and blasted, as if lightning had struck it or poison crept up from the roots. In its hollow trunk lay a giant egg, white as a peeled snail, and about as heavy as a man's heart.

"Don't touch that! Let it alone! It's mine!" shrieked Koschei crawling towards Ivan, his bony fingers slashing the air.

But Ivan lifted the egg over his head and hurled it to the ground, shattering the shell. A yellow, sulphorous, stinking yolk spilled out and scorched the grass for ever. With a scream of despair, Koschei rolled over . . . and disappeared. His body, his wickedness and all his magic evaporated in a jet of purple smoke. When Ivan looked around, not a demon or a goblin was to be seen. The statues in the grounds were stretching themselves, like sleepers waking.

With a creak of unoiled hinges, the gates of Castle Pitiless swung open. The shadows falling to north, south, east and west melted away, and all the sweet prisoners inside came running out.

There, moving like someone in a dream, was Princess Nadeshda, dressed as a bride. But instead of a flower in her hands, she held a single bright feather. She too had been visited by the Firebird.

The girls brought Ivan wedding clothes, and coronets of flowers for him and his bride. "Stay and make a home

in the castle, Prince. The sun shines in at the windows now.
And there's a whole kingdom without a ruler. Be our king
and Nadeshda can be our queen, and it shall be called
Castle Pitiless no longer, but Castle Ivan."

So Ivan and Nadeshda became the rulers of that
woodland kingdom. They renamed the castle 'Castle of
the Firebird'. Often, around sunset, when the western sky
turned red, a streak of scarlet flittered in and out of its
turrets, making red glints in the windows, swooping down
towards the river.

THE
SWANS AND THE
BRAVE PRINCESS

SAVIOUR PIROTTA

EMMA CHICHESTER CLARK

ONCE UPON A TIME, a king went hunting in a great forest. He was enjoying himself so much that he galloped on ahead, leaving his attendants far behind. Soon he was lost and, try as he might, could not find his way back to his people. He wandered among the trees, getting hungrier and more tired by the minute until, at last, he met an old woman.

"Can you show me the way out of the forest?" he asked her.

"I can help you, indeed," said the woman, who was really a witch, "but only on the condition that you take my daughter as your bride. She is beautiful and clever enough to be your queen."

The king had no choice but to agree, even though he was a widower and had no wish to marry again.

The witch led him to her hut and introduced him to

her daughter. The maiden was truly beautiful but there
was something cold and calculating about her, which
made the king very uneasy. Still, the king had given his
word that he would marry her, and a king never goes
back on a promise.

So he took the maiden by the hand and helped her up
onto his horse. The old witch pointed out the way and
before long, the king was at the edge of the forest, back
with his men. The very next day, he married the witch's
maiden and gave her beautiful chambers at the back of
the palace.

Now the king had seven children from his previous
marriage – six fine boys and a little girl. He was afraid
that his new wife might harm them, so he took them
to a castle in the middle of the forest and left them
there to be looked after by an old nanny. He came to
see them often but, as the castle was well hidden,

he could only find his way to it by using a magic ball of
wool. This ball had been given to him by a good fairy;
when he threw it on the ground it unravelled itself along
the forest path and showed him the way to his children.

It wasn't long before the new queen noticed that the
king went into the forest a great deal. She bribed some
of the servants, who told her about the children and how

they were hidden in the forest. They told her about the
magic ball of wool too, and how it helped the king find
the hidden castle. The queen became jealous of the
children and determined to get rid of them.

She made seven white shirts. Inside each shirt, she
sewed a magic charm. When the shirts were finished,
she used a magic mirror to find the secret ball of wool
and, in no time at all, was galloping on her horse towards
the children's hideout.

The children, who were expecting their father, rushed out to meet her. Only the youngest, the little girl, stayed behind in the castle. The queen hugged the boys and kissed them on the cheek; then she gave them the shirts. The boys tried them on and, as soon as the collars were fastened around their necks, they turned into swans and flew off into the sky. Delighted with her work, the wicked queen returned to the palace.

The next day the king came to visit his children. When he found the boys gone and his daughter clutching a handful of swan feathers, he thought that some forest spirit had put a spell on them. But he never for a moment suspected his new wife. Fuming with anger, he told the nanny to pack the girl's clothes, as he wanted to take her back to his palace with him. The little girl was not so keen

to meet her stepmother; she begged her father to let her
stay in the castle one more night and he agreed.

When the king and the nanny had gone to bed, the girl
said to herself, "I must find my brothers," and without any
more delay she set out into the forest. She walked and
walked until her feet could carry her no longer. Then,
quite by chance, she came upon a little hut. She went
inside and found six little beds, each one with a cotton
pillow. She dared not touch them, so she lay on the floor
and went to sleep.

At dusk, she was awoken by a rustling sound and six
swans came flying in through the open window. They
all settled on the floor and started flapping their wings.
Their feathers flew off their backs and and they turned
into boys. The girl realised they were her brothers and
was delighted to see them. But the boys said, "You mustn't

stay here a moment longer. This is a thieves' lair and if the crooks come back and find you here, they will kill you."

"Then you must look after me," said the girl.

"We can only stay for fifteen minutes," said her brothers. "After that we change into swans again."

"Is there nothing I can do to break the spell?" said the girl.

"No," said the boys, "the task is too hard; we would never ask you to suffer so for us."

"Tell me what to do," begged the girl.

"You must not talk or laugh for six years," said the boys. "And you must make us a shirt of starwort each. If you laugh but once or utter one single word, your efforts will have been in vain and we shall remain swans for ever."

"I'll free you," promised their sister. "Come back to me at the end of six years and I'll have the shirts ready."

The brothers nodded and, since the fifteen minutes were up, they turned into swans again. Their sister watched them fly away and then, by the light of the moon, she started looking for starwort. The next morning, she began making the shirts.

As the years went by, the girl grew into a young maiden. All alone in the forest, she worked at the shirts. Not a word or a sigh passed her lips, and she certainly did not feel like laughing. Never once did she stop stitching.

Now, one day, a handsome young prince came hunting in the forest and his servants found the young maiden sitting in a tree.

"Who are you?" they called.

The maiden did not reply but threw down her golden necklace. The servants called the prince and he climbed up

the tree and brought the maiden down in his arms. He asked her who she was in every language he knew but she never replied, nor did she smile. Still, the prince could not help noticing how beautiful she was and how well she carried herself. So he took her to his father's kingdom and made her his bride.

The prince's mother did not like the new princess at all. She spoke ill of her at every occasion and said to her friends, "It is very strange that she doesn't speak and that she keeps working away at that starwort. Who knows what evil powers she possesses?"

Some time later the princess had a baby. While she lay sleeping, the prince's mother crept to the cot and stole the child. Then she smeared hare's blood around the princess's mouth and, in the morning, said: "Look, the witch has devoured her own child."

The prince could not believe that his young wife would do such a thing. But a year later a second baby was born and it too disappeared. When the princess was again found with blood on her lips, his mother said: "Cast her out. She is evil."

"I'll give her one last chance," said the prince.

Soon a third child was born, and it too went the way of
the others. Now the prince confronted the princess, but she
would not say one word in her own defence; she merely
continued to stitch her shirts. The judge was called for and,
since the princess would not deny that she had killed her
own children, she was condemned to burn at the stake.

Now it so happened that the day the princess was to be
burned was also the last day of the six-year silence. The
princess had nearly finished sewing the shirts: there was
only the sleeve of one missing. When the soldiers came to
fetch her, she draped the six shirts over her arm and took
them with her to the place of execution. As she stood on
the pyre, the swans came flying towards her. She threw the
shirts over them and, in an instant, they were transformed
into young men. Only the sixth brother, who had been given
the unfinished shirt, was not completely changed: one of
his arms remained a swan's wing.

The brothers hugged their sister and she turned to the
prince and said, "Dearest husband, now that I can speak,
I can tell you that I am innocent. Your wicked mother stole
our babies and hid them." So it was that the children were
found and brought back to their happy parents, while the
prince's wicked mother was burned to death instead of
the young queen.

The six brothers sent word to their father to tell him that they were all safe and sound. Then they came to live in the palace with their sister, and they spent the rest of their lives in peace and happiness.

THE
PRINCESS AND THE PEA

ROSE IMPEY

IAN BECK

✸ ✸ ✸ ✸ ✸ ✸ ✸ ✸ ✸ ✸ ✸ ✸ ✸

ONCE UPON A TIME there was a prince who wanted to marry, so what did he do? He looked for a princess, of course. But she had to be a *real* princess. Nothing else would do. He travelled all over the world to find one, but without success.

There were plenty to choose from, at least, plenty who *said* they were real princesses. But the prince could never be sure.

There were no end of beautiful girls who put the sun to shame. There were any number of girls who could sing as sweetly as a bird and a dozen who could dance and wear out a pair of slippers in an evening. There were countless girls who were immensely rich and even more who had *been* rich, but were now terribly poor. There was no shortage of girls who had ugly sisters and cruel stepmothers. There were one or two girls who told him they'd been locked up in towers, and one who claimed she'd been asleep for a hundred years! There was even a girl who said she'd once kissed a frog. But no matter what they told him, the prince never knew whether to believe them. He could never be *absolutely* sure.

Finally the prince returned home, sad and disappointed, because he had so set his heart on finding a real princess.

His mother, the queen, hated to see her son so despondent.

"Don't worry, my dear. When the right girl comes along, I shall know how to tell. You leave it entirely to me."

One night there was a terrible storm in the city. The heavens opened and the rain fell in sheets like a waterfall. There was thunder and lightning. Something had upset the weather and now it was taking out its temper on the world.

Suddenly there was a loud knocking at the city gates and the king himself went to see who was there. When he opened the gates he saw a most forlorn and pathetic figure, who said she was a princess.

She was soaked to the skin. Her hair was dripping wet and hung like rats' tails. Her clothes were sticking to her, and even her shoes were awash with water. To be blunt about it, she looked like a poor, bedraggled creature, but she *said* she was a real princess.

And that was the truth – she was. She was presently on her travels around the world, in search of a prince. She was now old enough to marry and had set her heart on finding a *real* prince; nothing else would do. She had already met plenty who *said* they were real princes, but somehow she had a feeling they weren't.

There were no end of handsome young men who only had to be looked upon to be loved. There were any number of brave young men who had apparently slain dragons or demons or devils – some said with their bare hands. There were countless young men who had been turned into beasts, or birds, or frogs. There was even one young man who said he had hacked his way through a hedge, half a mile deep, to rescue a princess.

But no matter what they told her, the princess couldn't bring herself to believe them. She could never be *absolutely* sure.

And so here she was, still on her travels, feeling sad and disappointed. She had *so* set her heart on finding a real prince.

When the royal family first saw her, dripping on the palace floors, they were not easily convinced either. How could they tell if she were a real princess, the state she was in? The poor prince was as confused as ever. But the queen knew exactly what to do.

"Come with me," she told him. "We'll soon find out."

They went together to the bedchamber, where the princess was to sleep. The queen told the prince to take the mattress off the bed. Then she laid a single pea on the base of the bed. On top of it, they laid twenty mattresses. And then, on top of those, they laid twenty feather beds. And that was the bed the princess was to sleep in.

All through the night the princess lay awake. She tossed and she turned. She wriggled and she jiggled in the bed to try to make herself more comfortable, but it was no use. By morning she was perfectly miserable.

When she came down to breakfast, the queen asked,
"Did you sleep well, my dear?"

But the princess replied, "No, I'm afraid I didn't. In fact,
I hardly closed my eyes. I don't know when I've had such
a bad night's sleep. There must have been something in
the bed, because this morning I am covered in bruises.
How I have suffered!"

And then the prince *knew* that she must be a real princess. Who else could have felt a single pea through twenty mattresses and twenty feather beds? Only a real princess would be so sensitive.

"For years, I have been looking for a real princess," said the prince. "Now that I've found you, will you marry me?"

The princess considered this carefully. If he could know with such certainty that she was a *real* princess, which she was, then surely it must follow that he was indeed a *real* prince too. (And he was.)

Now, when a real and handsome prince meets a real and beautiful princess, it's only natural that he should ask her to marry him. And what could be more natural than for her to accept? So she did.

And what should they both do then? Why, live happily ever after, of course. And they did.

And so, I hope, will you.

THE
END

ABOUT THE AUTHORS

ROSE IMPEY is highly regarded as a writer for children of all ages. She has a deep love and an extensive knowledge of fairy and folk tales, and her titles include *The Orchard Book of Fairy Tales* and the internationally successful *Titchy Witch* series.

MARGARET MAYO has a love of myth and folk tales, and a deep and wide-ranging knowledge of their sources. She has written many highly-acclaimed collections for children, including *First Fairy Tales* and *The Orchard Book of the Unicorn and Other Magical Animals*.

GERALDINE McCAUGHREAN has gained countless awards, including the Carnegie Medal and the Whitbread Children's Book Award. She has written the official sequel to J.M. Barrie's *Peter Pan*. Her other titles include *The Orchard Book of Greek Myths*.

SAVIOUR PIROTTA has won the English Association Award and is the author of numerous books for children, ranging from collections of folk tales to gift books and fiction titles. His work for Orchard includes *The Sleeping Princess and Other Fairy Tales from Grimm*.

About the Illustrators

ANGELA BARRETT is one of today's leading children's book illustrators, whose art is acclaimed throughout the world. She has won the Smarties Prize and the WH Smith Award. Her work includes *The Orchard Book of Shakespeare Stories*.

IAN BECK is among the country's best-loved creators of children's books and his illustrations also appear frequently in magazines. He has been shortlisted for The Best Books for Babies Award. His titles include *The Orchard Book of Fairy Tales* and *Peter Pan and Wendy*.

EMMA CHICHESTER CLARK is a celebrated illustrator, loved the world over. She has won the prestigious Mother Goose Award and has been shortlisted for the Kate Greenaway Medal. Her titles include *The Orchard Book of Aesop's Fables*.

JANE RAY is a prestigious children's illustrator, whose work is well known across the world. She has won the Smarties Prize and has been shortlisted five times for the Kate Greenaway Medal. Her many books for Orchard include *The Apple-Pip Princess*.

ACKNOWLEDGEMENTS

Orchard Books would like to thank the following for the use of copyright material in this collection. All books cited are published by Orchard Books.

CINDERELLA
from *The Orchard Book of Stories from the Ballet*
Text © Geraldine McCaughrean 1994
Illustrations © Angela Barrett 1994

THE MAGIC BEAR AND THE HANDSOME PRINCE
from *The Sleeping Princess and Other Fairy Tales from Grimm*
Text © Saviour Pirotta 2002
Illustrations © Emma Chichester Clark 2002

THE PRINCE AND THE FLYING CARPET
from *The Orchard Book of Magical Tales*
Text © Margaret Mayo 1993
Illustrations © Jane Ray 1993

BEAUTY AND THE BEAST
from *The Orchard Book of Fairy Tales*
Text © Rose Impey 1992
Illustrations © Ian Beck 1992
Reproduced by permission of The Agency (London) Ltd
on behalf of Ian Beck

THE FIREBIRD
from *The Orchard Book of Stories from the Ballet*
Text © Geraldine McCaughrean 1994
Illustrations © Angela Barrett 1994

THE SWANS AND THE BRAVE PRINCESS
from *The Sleeping Princess and Other Fairy Tales from Grimm*
Text © Saviour Pirotta 2002
Illustrations © Emma Chichester Clark 2002

THE PRINCESS AND THE PEA
from *The Orchard Book of Fairy Tales*
Text © Rose Impey 1992
Illustrations © Ian Beck 1992
Reproduced by permission of The Agency (London) Ltd
on behalf of Ian Beck

FRONT AND BACK COVER AND SPINE VIGNETTES:

from CINDERELLA and THE FIREBIRD from *The Orchard Book of Stories from the Ballet*
Illustrations © Angela Barrett 1994

JACKET FRONT FLAP VIGNETTES:

from BEAUTY AND THE BEAST from *The Orchard Book of Fairy Tales*
Illustration © Ian Beck 1992
Reproduced by permission of The Agency (London) Ltd on behalf of Ian Beck

from THE PRINCE AND THE FLYING CARPET from *The Orchard Book of Magical Tales*
Illustration © Jane Ray 1993

JACKET BACK FLAP VIGNETTES:

from CINDERELLA from *The Orchard Book of Stories from the Ballet*
Illustration © Angela Barrett 1994

from THE SWANS AND THE BRAVE PRINCESS
from *The Sleeping Princess and Other Fairy Tales from Grimm*
Illustration © Emma Chichester Clark 2002